P9-BYP-137

M	marsh mask milkweed mist moon mosquito moth mouse mouth mushrooms
N	naked nasturtium navel nest net nightingale nixie nose nuts
O	oak ocean on orange owl
P	pack paddle pan peaks pear perch percolator pie pineapple pinecone pine trees plaid plum pond porcupine
Q	queen Queen Anne's lace quilt quince
R	rabbit race rain raincoat ribbon roller skates roses
S	sail sand sandal scallop sea seagull sea urchin seaweed shell sit spine starfish stick sun sunglasses swimsuit
T	table tablecloth tail talk teacup teapot teeth telephones thread ties toe top topknots tulips turtle twins twist two
U	umbrella uncombed under underwear upon ups-a-daisies
V	valentine valley vegetables vest village violets violin
W	wade water water lily weather vane weeds wheel wheelbarrow whistle wind windmill wings wood wren
X	xxx
Y	yarn yarrow yawn yellow jackets Yorkshire terrier
Z	zinnia zipper zoo

A
LITTLE
ALPHABET

Merry Christmas Pat!

Trina Schart Hyman

1993

A LITTLE ALPHABET

BY
TRINA SCHART HYMAN

BOOKS OF WONDER
WILLIAM MORROW & COMPANY
NEW YORK

Pen and ink and watercolors were used for the full-color art.

Copyright © 1980, 1993 by Trina Schart Hyman
Originally published in two colors by Little, Brown and Company,
Boston, 1980.
William Morrow and Company, Inc.,
1350 Avenue of the Americas, New York, NY 10019 or
Books of Wonder, 132 Seventh Avenue at 18th Street, New York, NY 10011.
Printed in the United States of America.
1 2 3 4 5 6 7 8 9 10
Library of Congress Cataloging-in-Publication Data
Hyman, Trina Schart. A little alphabet / by Trina Schart Hyman.   p.   cm. —
(Books of wonder) Originally published: Boston : Little, Brown, c1980.
Summary: Each letter of the alphabet is illustrated with a boy or girl playing
with or using objects beginning with that letter.
ISBN 0-688-12034-2.
1. English language—Alphabet—Juvenile literature. [1. Alphabet.]
I. Title. II. Series. PE1155.H9 1993 421′.1—dc20 [E]
92-29692 CIP AC

Books of Wonder is a registered trademark of Ozma, Inc.

A	*acorns anemone ant apples apron arm artichoke artist avocado*
B	*barefoot basket beehive bees berries bird boy brambles brow buckle*
C	*cage cake canary candle cape cat checks cheek clouds collar cricket crocus curls*
D	*daffodil daisies dandelion dig dirt dog dragonfly dungarees*
E	*ear Easter basket eat egg eggcup elbow evening primrose eye eyebrow*
F	*feather fern fingers fins fish fishing pole fist float fly foot frayed frog pond*
G	*geranium girl glass gnome goose grapes grapevine grasp grass*
H	*halter hat hawk hay hole honeysuckle horse house*
I	*ice ice skates icicles ink island*
J	*jacks jam jaw Johnny-jump-ups jump jumper jump rope juniper*
K	*kerchief kettle keyhole keys king's trefoil kitten knees knock*
L	*lace ladybug lantern lashes leaf lean lemon lick lily lime lips lizard lollipop*